The Art Show Mystery

By Eleanor Robins

Development: Kent Publishing Services, Inc.
Design and Production: Signature Design Group, Inc.
Illustrations: Jan Naimo Jones

SADDLEBACK
EDUCATIONAL PUBLISHING
www.sdlback.com

ISBN-13: 978-1-59905-027-0
ISBN-10: 1-59905-027-7
e-book ISBN: 978-1-60291-456-8

Printed in the United States of America

15 14 13 12 11   5 6 7 8 9

Chapter 1

It was Monday. Paige was on her way to art class. Miss Brock was her art teacher.

Steve walked with Paige. He was in the class, too.

Paige and Steve were good friends. They both lived at Grayson Apartments. And they rode the same bus to school.

"Did you finish your painting, Steve?" Paige asked.

"No. But I will today," Steve said.

"I hope I can finish my painting today," Paige said.

But she wasn't sure she would. She wanted to do a lot more to it.

"I want to put my painting in the art show," Paige said.

The art show was this Friday.

"What about you, Steve? Are you going to put your painting in the art show?" Paige asked.

"Not me. I don't want people to talk about my painting," Steve said.

Paige didn't know why Steve felt that way. She wanted people to look at her painting. And she wanted them to talk about it, too.

Paige and Steve got to the art room. They went into the room.

The bell rang. It was time for class to start.

Miss Brock said, "All of you need to work hard. The art show is this Friday. Try to finish your paintings today. Then we can start to get ready for the art show tomorrow."

Steve asked, "Do I have to put my painting in the art show?"

"No, Steve. But I hope you will put your work in the show. I hope all of you do," Miss Brock said.

But Paige didn't think Steve would.

Paige put her books down. She walked over to her painting. It was next to Kay's painting.

Paige looked at Kay's painting.

Paige said, "I like your painting."

"Thanks," Kay said.

But Kay didn't say that she liked Paige's painting.

Paige picked up her paintbrush. She was ready to work on her painting.

Miss Brock said, "Time to start. Work hard."

Paige worked on her painting for a long time.

Then Miss Brock said, "You need to save some time to clean up. So you have only ten more minutes to work."

Paige thought her painting was good. She hoped Miss Brock would think it was, too.

Miss Brock asked, "Have you finished your painting, Paige?"

"Not yet, Miss Brock," Paige said.

Miss Brock walked over to Paige. She looked at Paige's painting.

Then she said, "I like your painting, Paige. It is very nice."

"Thank you, Miss Brock," she said.

Paige was glad Miss Brock liked her painting. She hoped other people would, too.

Miss Brock said, "I hope you put your painting in the art show, Paige. Then everyone can see it."

"Oh, yes, Miss Brock. I sure will," Paige said.

Maybe she would win a prize, too. That would be great.

Chapter 2

It was the next day. Paige was on her way to art class. Steve walked with her.

"I hope I finish my painting today," Paige said.

"Do you still want to put it in the art show?" Steve asked.

Paige said, "Yes. I hope I can win a prize. You have seen my painting, Steve. Do you think I can win a prize?"

Steve stopped to talk to Mr. Nash. And he didn't answer Paige.

Paige stopped to talk to Mr. Nash, too.

Mr. Nash cleaned the school. And sometimes he fixed things.

Mr. Nash was at the classroom next to the art room. He had just put new numbers on the door.

Steve asked, "Why did you put new numbers on the door, Mr. Nash?"

"Mr. Glenn told me to do it."

Mr. Glenn was the principal.

"What about the other doors? Are you going to put new numbers on them, too?" Steve asked.

"Maybe I will. Maybe Mr. Ross will," Mr. Nash said.

Mr. Ross worked at the school, too.

Steve said, "The old numbers are OK. Why does Mr. Glenn want to change them?"

"Don't ask me. Ask Mr. Glenn," Mr. Nash said.

"The new numbers look better than the old numbers," Paige said.

"But the old numbers were OK. So why change them?" Steve asked.

The bell rang. Paige and Steve hurried into the art room. It was time for class to start.

Miss Brock said, "A few of you still need to finish your artwork. And you need to do it quickly."

"Why?" Steve asked.

Miss Brock said, "Mr. Glenn came to see your artwork this morning. He said your artwork is very good. And he said all of your artwork must be moved to Room 19."

That surprised Paige. She thought the art show would be in the art room.

Steve said, "Why do we have to move our artwork? I thought the show would be in here."

Miss Brock said, "It will be. But Mr. Glenn wants everything moved out of here. Then Mr. Nash and Mr. Ross can clean the room."

"When will they clean the room?" Paige asked.

Miss Brock said, "They will clean the room tomorrow. So we will meet in Room 127. Then on Thursday you can begin to move your artwork back in here. And we will get ready for the art show."

"When do you want us to move our artwork today?" Paige asked.

Miss Brock said, "I hope you can take it to Room 19 before art class is over."

Steve said, "I don't want my work in the art show. Can I take it home today? Or do you want me to take it to Room 19?"

Steve's painting wasn't very big. So he could take it home on the bus.

"I will grade it today, Steve. Then you can take it home," Miss Brock said.

Miss Brock told two boys to take their artwork to Room 19. She gave one of them a key to the door.

Miss Brock said, "Put your artwork in there. Then lock the door. And bring the key back to me."

Paige worked on her painting.

It wasn't long until the two boys were back. More students moved their artwork. And time went by quickly.

At last the was painting finished. Paige thought it was very good.

Kay walked over to Paige. She looked at the painting.

Kay asked, "Did you finish your painting, Paige?"

"Yes," Paige said.

"Are you going to put it in the art show?" Kay asked.

"Yes. I hope that I win a prize," Paige said.

"I wouldn't count on it," Kay said.

Paige quickly put the paint away. And she cleaned her paintbrush.

Then she was ready to take her painting to Room 19.

Why did Kay say that? Paige wanted to ask her. But the bell rang. It was time for class to be over.

Paige needed to go to her next class.

It was too late to take her painting to Room 19.

Paige went over to Miss Brock.

Paige said, "I don't have time to take my painting to Room 19. What am I going to do?"

"Come by my room some time today. And you can take your painting then. You can borrow my key to Room 19," Miss Brock said.

But Paige didn't have any free time for the rest of the day. She had a math test. And she had to study some more for it. Paige had to do that during part of her lunch time. So she couldn't take her painting then.

When would she have time to take her painting to Room 19?

Chapter 3

Paige was in her math class. Mr. Wang was her teacher.

Paige worked hard on her math test. She wanted to finish early. Then maybe Mr. Wang would let her go to the art class. And she could take her painting to Room 19.

Paige finished the math test. Then she checked her answers. She thought she had done a good job on the test.

She took the test to Mr. Wang.

"Is it OK for me to leave early? I have to go to the art room. I need to get my painting. And I have to take it to Room 19," Paige said.

Mr. Wang knew about the art show. And he knew the students had to move their artwork.

"Did you check your answers, Paige?" Mr. Wang asked.

Paige said, "Yes, Mr. Wang. And I think I did well on my test."

"Then you can go, Paige. But take all of your books with you," he said.

"Thanks, Mr. Wang," Paige said.

Paige got her books. And she hurried to the art room. She knew she didn't have much time.

Paige saw Mr. Nash. He was sweeping the floor outside the art room.

"Hi, Mr. Nash," Paige said.

Then Paige went into the art room.

Most of the artwork was gone. But not all of it.

Paige looked for Miss Brock. But it was her planning time. And Miss Brock wasn't there. So Paige couldn't borrow her key.

Paige went back into the hall. She walked over to Mr. Nash.

"Do you know where Miss Brock is?" Paige asked.

Maybe Miss Brock was somewhere near by. Then Paige could get the key.

"I don't know," Mr. Nash said.

"I need to take my painting to Room 19. And the room is locked. Miss Brock said I could borrow her key. But she isn't here. So I can't get her key. Can I borrow your keys?" Paige asked.

Mr. Nash had many keys on a key ring.

"Sorry. I can't let you do that," Mr. Nash said.

"But I will bring them right back. And I won't unlock any other room," Paige said.

"I can't let you borrow them. Or I would have to let all of the students borrow them. I sure can't do that," Mr. Nash said.

What was Paige going to do? She had to move her painting. And this was the only time she had to do it.

Mr. Nash said, "Tell you what I will do. I will go with you. And I will unlock the door for you."

"Thanks, Mr. Nash. That is very nice of you," Paige said.

Paige hurried back into the art room. She got her painting. Then she went out into the hall.

It was hard to carry both her painting and her books.

"Need some help? I'd be glad to carry the painting for you," Mr. Nash said.

"Thanks," Paige said.

She gave the painting to Mr. Nash.

The two quickly went down the hall to Room 19.

Paige saw Mr. Ross. He had just put new numbers on one of the doors. Some doors already had new numbers.

Paige saw room 19. New numbers were on the door. Paige stopped and looked at the door.

"This is the room," Paige said.

"Are you sure this is the right room?" Mr. Nash asked.

"Yes," Paige said.

"Are you really sure about that?" Mr. Nash asked.

Paige said, "Yes. This is the room Miss Brock said to put it in."

Mr. Nash put the painting on the floor. He unlocked the door. Then he took the painting into the room.

Mr. Nash asked, "Where do you want me to put your painting?"

Paige showed him where to put the painting. And Mr. Nash put it there.

Then the two of them went out into the hall. And Mr. Nash locked the door.

"Thanks for the help, Mr. Nash," Paige said.

Then Paige hurried to her next class. She didn't want to be late.

Her painting was in Room 19 now. And she didn't have to worry any more about it.

Chapter 4

It was Thursday. Paige hurried into the art room. Steve was already there. It was almost time for art class to start.

"The art room looks very nice, Miss Brock," Paige said.

The floor was very clean. The tables had white tablecloths on them. Some tables had artwork on them, too.

The bell rang.

Miss Brock said, "You can help me get ready for the art show. Or you can draw or use this class as a study time."

Paige wanted to help Miss Brock get ready for the art show.

Miss Brock said, "You can go to Room 19. Two at a time. Get your artwork and bring it back here. Be quiet on the way. And don't forget, lock the room when you leave."

Miss Brock picked two students to go to Room 19 first. She gave one of them her key to the room.

Paige looked at Steve.

Paige asked, "What are you going to do, Steve?"

"I need to study. So I guess I will study," Steve said.

"I will help Miss Brock," Paige said.

"Who wants to help me get ready for the show?" Miss Brock asked.

"I do," Paige said.

"So do I," Kay said.

Some other students said they wanted to help, too.

Paige started to help Miss Brock. Other students went to get their artwork, two at a time.

The class time went by quickly.

Then Miss Brock said, "Paige, you need to get your artwork. And you need to hurry. It is almost time for class to be over. Kay, you go with Paige."

Miss Brock gave Kay the key to unlock the door.

Paige and Kay went out into the hall. They were the last two to get their artwork.

They started to walk quickly to Room 19.

They got to the hall that Room 19 was on. Kay stopped in front of a door.

Kay said, "Good. We are here."

Paige was surprised. She didn't think she and Mr. Nash put her painting in this room.

"Are you sure this is the room?" Paige asked.

Kay said, "Yes. I put my painting in this room. Look on the door. And you will see this is the right room."

Paige looked at the numbers on the door. They were one and nine. So it must be the right room.

Kay unlocked the door.

Paige and Kay went into the room.

Paige said, "This doesn't look like the right room to me."

"It does to me. You just forgot where you put your painting," Kay said.

But how could Paige forget where she put her painting?

Some of the artwork was back in the art room. Maybe that was why the room didn't look the same to her.

Kay hurried over to her painting. She picked it up.

Then Kay said, "We need to get back to class. So hurry and get your painting, Paige."

Paige looked at where she thought her painting would be.

But her painting wasn't there. Had someone moved it?

Chapter 5

Paige walked around the room. Only a few paintings were in the room. She looked at all of them.

Her painting had to be there. But it wasn't there.

Kay said, "I have my painting. Hurry and get your painting, Paige. We need to go back to the art room. It is almost time for our next class."

"My painting is gone," Paige said.

Kay didn't look surprised that Paige said that.

"Are you sure?" Kay asked.

"Yes. I am sure," Paige said.

"Did you look at all of the paintings?" Kay asked.

"Yes," Paige said.

"Are you sure you put your painting in here? Maybe you did put it in some other room," Kay said.

"I put it in Room 19. And this is Room 19," Paige said.

"Maybe Miss Brock knows where it is," Kay said.

Miss Brock sent Paige to Room 19 to get the painting. So Paige didn't think Miss Brock knew where it was.

But maybe Miss Brock did know. And she just forgot to tell Paige.

"Maybe you should look some more in here. But we need to get back to the art room. We can't be late to our next class," Kay said.

Paige didn't want to go to her next class. She wanted to look for her painting. But she didn't know where to look for it.

It wasn't in Room 19. She was sure about that.

The girls went out to the hall.

Kay had her painting. So Paige locked the door.

The bell rang.

Paige and Kay walked quickly.

When they got back to the art room, Steve and most of the other students had gone to the next class.

Kay put her painting on a table.

Miss Brock asked, "Where is your painting, Paige?"

"It wasn't in Room 19. And I don't know where it is. Do you know where it is?" Paige asked.

"No, Paige. Are you sure it wasn't in Room 19?" Miss Brock asked.

"Yes," Paige said.

"Kay, did you help Paige look for it?" Miss Brock asked.

Kay said, "No, Miss Brock. We had to hurry back here. So I didn't have time to help Paige."

But Kay didn't need to help her look. The painting wasn't in Room 19.

"Where could it be, Miss Brock?" Paige asked.

"I don't know, Paige," she said.

"Do you think someone moved it?" Paige asked.

"No, Paige. I don't know how someone could have moved it. The room was locked. And the person would need a key," Miss Brock said.

But most of the students in Paige's class had been to Room 19. The students in some other art classes had been there, too. They all had a key to unlock the door, so they could get their own work.

Did someone in her class take the painting? Or did someone in one of the other classes take it?

But why?

Paige needed to go to her next class. So she went to get her books. Kay went to get her books, too.

Kay said, "I am sure you will find your painting, Paige. But it might be after the art show."

Then Kay hurried out of the room.

Why did Kay say that? Did she take the painting?

But why? Was it because she thought Paige might win a prize?

Maybe Kay did take the painting. But when did Kay take it?

And where did Kay put Paige's painting?

Chapter 6

It was lunch time. Paige hurried into the lunchroom. She was still very upset. She quickly got her lunch. Then she looked for her friends.

Paige saw Steve. Steve was at a table with Carl, Jack, Lin, and Gail.

Paige hurried over to their table and sat down.

Steve said, "You don't look so good, Paige. What is wrong with you?"

"Yeah. What is wrong with you?" Carl asked.

"My painting is missing," Paige said.

"Are you sure?" Lin asked.

"Yes. Do you think someone took it?" Paige asked.

Paige thought Kay took it. But she didn't know that for sure. So she didn't want to say anything.

Steve laughed.

"Why did you laugh? It isn't funny," Paige said.

"Sorry. I couldn't help it. I have seen your painting. And believe me about this, Paige. No one would steal it. It isn't that good," Steve said.

"That wasn't nice, Steve," Gail said.

"For sure," Jack said.

"Sorry. But it is true," Steve said.

"OK. So maybe you don't like my painting. But Miss Brock said it is very nice," Paige said.

Steve laughed again.

Then he said, "Sorry. I couldn't help it, Paige."

"Now what is so funny?" she asked.

"Miss Brock tells all the students their artwork is nice. She even says that to me. And you know how bad my artwork is," Steve said.

"Steve is teasing you, Paige. Don't let him upset you," Gail said.

Gail was being nice. But Paige knew Steve wasn't joking with her. That was what he really thought.

Maybe her painting wasn't that good. And maybe she wouldn't win a prize in the show. And maybe Kay didn't take her painting after all.

But where was her painting?

Lin asked, "How do you know the painting is gone, Paige? Did Miss Brock say it is?"

"No. She sent me to get it. And I couldn't find it. It was gone," Paige said.

"Maybe you didn't look in the right room for it," Carl said.

Jack said, "Yes. Maybe you didn't look in the right room for it."

"I put my painting in Room 19. So it had to be in that room," Paige said.

"Maybe someone moved your painting," Steve said.

"Someone moved it," Jack said.

"But where is it?" Paige asked.

"Don't worry, Paige. We will help you find it," Gail said.

"Yes, Paige. We will help you find it," Lin said.

"For sure," Jack said.

Gail looked at Steve and Carl.

Then Gail said, "All of us will help."

"Yes. All of us," Carl said.

"Yeah," said Steve.

They were her friends. So Paige was sure that they would help her solve the mystery.

But could they help her find her painting before the art show?

Chapter 7

Paige tried to eat. But she kept thinking about her painting.

"Cheer up, Paige. It is only a lost painting," Steve said.

"That wasn't nice, Steve. The painting means a lot to Paige. And we have to find it," Gail said.

"What can I do to help? Just say the word. And I will do it," Jack said.

Paige said, "I don't know. I just know we have to find my painting."

"We can ask around. Maybe someone has seen it," Carl said.

"But the art show is tomorrow," Paige said.

Lin said, "I wish we could all look for the painting. But we can't do it now. And we have to ride the bus home. So we can't stay after school."

"Just say the word. And I will take you home," Jack said.

Jack was the only one who had a car. It wasn't much of a car. But it was still a car. Jack liked to show it off. So he was always glad to take them somewhere.

"How, Jack? You don't have your car at school," Steve said.

"I will ride the bus home. And then I will come back in my car. And I will take you home," Jack said.

"Great idea, Jack," Gail said.

"That sounds like a plan," Carl said.

"Thanks, Jack. It is very nice of you to do that," Paige said.

"Where should we meet after school?" Lin asked.

"Let's meet outside the art room," Paige said.

Paige thought that was the best place to meet. Then she could talk to Miss Brock. Maybe Miss Brock had heard something about her painting.

Gail said, "Just one thing. I have to work today. So I can't stay after school."

Gail wanted to be a librarian. So she worked at the town library some days after school and some weekends.

Carl said, "I have football practice. And you know I can't be late to that. So I can't help after school."

Carl was on the football team. He was the quarterback.

"But Steve and I can still help, right Steve?" Lin asked.

Lin looked hopefully at Steve.

"Right. I guess I can help," Steve said.

"And I will help when I get back to school," Jack said.

"I hope we have found my painting by then," Paige said.

"Don't worry, Paige. We will have found it by then," Lin said.

But Lin didn't look like she believed that. And the other four didn't look like they believed that either.

Chapter 8

Paige was in her last class of the day. Jack was in the class, too.

The end of school bell rang. Paige was glad. Now she could look for her painting.

Jack came over to Paige.

Jack said, "I will be back as soon as I can."

"Thanks, Jack. But don't drive too fast," Paige said.

"Never," Jack said.

Paige believed him. He cared too much about his car to drive too fast.

Jack hurried out of the classroom.

Paige quickly picked up her books. Then she hurried to the art room.

Steve and Lin were waiting for her outside the door.

"What should we do first, Paige?" Steve asked.

"We should talk to Miss Brock. Maybe she has heard something about my painting," Paige said.

They went into the art room. The room was almost ready for the art show.

"Look at the great artwork, Steve," Lin said.

Steve said, "Yeah. And look how clean the art room is."

Paige saw Miss Brock.

"Have you found my painting, Miss Brock? Or have you heard something about it?" Paige asked.

Miss Brock said, "No, Paige. But maybe it is in Room 19. And you just didn't see it. Maybe you should look there again."

"Good idea," Steve said.

Did Steve think the painting was there? Did he think she didn't know her own painting?

"I have a key to the room, Paige. You can borrow it," Miss Brock said.

Miss Brock gave the key to Paige.

Paige said, "Thanks, Miss Brock. I will bring it back as soon as I can."

Then Paige hurried to Room 19. Steve and Lin were with her.

"I know my painting isn't in there. I have already looked there," Paige said.

"It won't hurt to look again, Paige," Lin said.

Paige unlocked the door. And they went in. Some artwork was in the room. But not very much.

The three looked around the room. But they didn't see Paige's painting.

"Are you sure you put your painting in here?" Steve asked.

Paige was starting to get very mad at Steve.

"I put my painting in Room 19. And this is Room 19," Paige said.

Steve walked out into the hall. He looked at the room number.

Then he said, "Yeah. It sure is. But maybe you didn't put your painting in Room 19 after all."

"I did," Paige almost yelled at Steve.

Paige looked down the hall. She saw Mr. Nash.

"You can ask Mr. Nash. He unlocked the door for me. And he put my painting in the room. He can tell you it was Room 19," Paige said.

"OK. I will ask him," Steve said.

Paige just said that to Steve. She didn't think he would ask Mr. Nash.

Steve walked over to Mr. Nash. Paige and Lin did, too.

Paige said, "You unlocked the door for me, Mr. Nash. And you put my painting in the room. It was Room 19, right?"

"It sure was," Mr. Nash said.

Paige looked at Steve.

Paige said, "I told you it was."

"That day it was," Mr. Nash said.

"What does that mean, Mr. Nash?" Steve asked.

"That day it was Room 19. Today it is Room 15," Mr. Nash said.

Paige couldn't believe what Mr. Nash had just said.

"How could that be?" Paige asked.

"Mr. Ross put the wrong numbers on some of the doors. I had to change them this morning," Mr. Nash said.

"That is why you can't find your painting. It is in Room 15," Steve said.

Steve started to laugh.

Mr. Nash said, "I will unlock Room 15 for you. Your painting should be in there. That is the room we put it in."

Mr. Nash went to Room 15. Paige and Steve went with him. Lin did, too.

Mr. Nash unlocked the door.

Paige hurried into the room. She quickly found her missing painting. It hadn't been missing after all.

"Great, Paige. It is here," Lin said.

The painting might not win a prize. But Paige was glad she found it.

Paige looked at Steve. He was laughing again.

"OK, Steve. I was wrong this time. But that is the only time I was wrong," Paige said.

Then she started to laugh, too.